The Editorial Staff of

The Rodent's Gazette

1. Linda Thinslice
2. Sweetie Cheesetriangle
3. Ratella Redfur
4. Soya Mousehao
5. Cheesita de la Pampa
6. Mouseanna Mousetti
7. Yale Youngmouse
8. Toni Tinypaw
9. Tina Spicytail
10. Maximilian Mousemower
11. Valerie Vole
12. Trap Stilton
13. Branwen Musclemouse
14. Zeppola Zap
15. Merenguita Gingermouse
16. Ratsy O'Shea
17. Rodentrick Roundrat
18. Teddy von Muffler
19. Thea Stilton
20. Erronea Misprint
21. Pinky Pick
22. Ya-ya O'Cheddar
23. Mousella MacMouser
24. Kreamy O'Cheddar
25. Blasco Tabasco
26. Toffie Sugarsweet
27. Tylerat Truemouse
28. Larry Keys
29. Michael Mouse
30. Geronimo Stilton
31. Benjamin Stilton
32. Briette Finerat
33. Raclette Finerat

Geronimo Stilton
A learned and brainy
mouse; editor of
The Rodent's Gazette

Thea Stilton
Geronimo's sister and
special correspondent at
The Rodent's Gazette

Trap Stilton
An awful joker;
Geronimo's cousin and
owner of the store
Cheap Junk for Less

Benjamin Stilton
A sweet and loving
nine-year-old mouse;
Geronimo's favorite
nephew

Dear mouse friends,
welcome to the world of

Geronimo Stilton

Geronimo Stilton

FOUR MICE DEEP in the JUNGLE

PUFFIN

PUFFIN BOOKS

Published by the Penguin Group
Penguin Books Ltd, 80 Strand, London WC2R 0RL, England
Penguin Group (USA) Inc., 375 Hudson Street, New York, New York 10014, USA
Penguin Group (Canada), 90 Eglinton Avenue East, Suite 700, Toronto, Ontario, Canada M4P 2Y3
(a division of Pearson Penguin Canada Inc.)
Penguin Ireland, 25 St Stephen's Green, Dublin 2, Ireland (a division of Penguin Books Ltd)
Penguin Group (Australia), 250 Camberwell Road, Camberwell, Victoria 3124, Australia
(a division of Pearson Australia Group Pty Ltd)
Penguin Books India Pvt Ltd, 11 Community Centre, Panchsheel Park, New Delhi – 110 017, India
Penguin Group (NZ), 67 Apollo Drive, Rosedale, Auckland 0632, New Zealand
(a division of Pearson New Zealand Ltd)
Penguin Books (South Africa) (Pty) Ltd, Block D, Rosebank Office Park, 181 Jan Smuts Avenue, Parktown
North, Gauteng 2193, South Africa

Penguin Books Ltd, Registered Offices: 80 Strand, London WC2R 0RL, England

puffinbooks.com

English-language edition first published in Great Britain by Scholastic Children's Books 2004
This edition published in Great Britain in Puffin Books 2012
001 – 10 9 8 7 6 5 4 3 2 1

Geronimo Stilton names, characters and related indicia are copyright, trademark and exclusive
license of Atlantyca S.p.A. All Rights Reserved.
The moral right of the author and illustrator has been asserted

Text by Geronimo Stilton
Original cover by Lorenzo Chiavini
Illustrations by Lorenzo Chiavini, revised by Chiara Sacchi, Flavio Ferron and Silvia Bigolin
Graphics by Merenguita Gingermouse, Francesco Marconi and Gioia Giunchi
Special thanks to Kathryn Cristaldi
Original cover design by Ursula Albano
Interior layout by Kay Petronio

Text, illustrations and English translation copyright © 2000, 2004,
Edizioni Piemme S.p.A., via Tiziano 32 - 20145 Milano – Italy
International Rights copyright © Atlantyca S.p.A., via Leopardi 8, 20123 Milano - Italy

Original title: *Quattro Topi Nella Giungla Nera*
Based on an original idea by Elisabetta Dami
www.geronimostilton.com

*Stilton is the name of a famous English cheese. It is a registered trademark of the
Stilton Cheesemakers' Association. For more information go to www.stiltoncheese.com*

Without limiting the rights under copyright reserved above, no part of this book may be stored,
reproduced or transmitted in any form or by any means, electronic or mechanical, including photocopying,
recording, or by any information storage and retrieval system, without written permission from the
copyright holder. For information address Atlantyca S.p.A., via Leopardi 8, 20123 Milano,
Italy - foreignrights@atlantyca.it - www.atlantyca.com

British Library Cataloguing in Publication Data
A CIP catalogue record for this book is available from the British Library

ISBN: 978–0–141–34131–6

Printed by Graphicom, Italy

www.greenpenguin.co.uk

How Serious Is It, Dr. Shrinkfur?

I was lying on the psychiatrist's couch. It was made of soft, fluffy cat fur. But I wasn't very comfortable. I was worried.

"How serious is it, Dr. Shrinkfur?" I murmured, chewing my whiskers.

The doctor leaned back in his chair. "Ach, first I haff to know more," he squeaked in his funny accent. "Vhen did zis thing start?"

I sighed. I was never the bravest mouse on the block. In fact, I guess you could say

BOO!

I've always been a bit of a 'fraidy mouse. I've never enjoyed spooky holidays like Halloween. I hide in my mouse hole on the

1

Fourth of July. Fireworks make me nervous. But lately, it seemed like everything was making me jumpy. "Well, at first I was only afraid to go to the dentist, but then I suddenly became afraid of ↑ELEVATORS↓. Then came the fear of flying. That was followed by a fear of spiders, snakes, closed spaces, and crowds. After that I became afraid of heights and the dark." I took a deep breath. Just talking about all of my fears was making me afraid! "Oh, yes, I almost forgot, Doctor," I added. "I'm also afraid of *cats*!"

Dr. Shrinkfur waved his paw.

"You are a mouse, you haff to be afraid of *cats*!" he said.

I TWIRLED MY TAIL NERVOUSLY. Then I sat up. "Please, Dr. Shrinkfur," I squeaked. "Give it to me straight."

He shook his head solemnly. "Vell, zis could be serious," he began. "Or it could not be. Zis is up to you!"

I scratched my head. "Well, is the cure going to take long?" I asked.

The doctor jotted down some notes on a pad. "Vell, it could be long," he said. "Or it could not be long. Zis is up to you!"

Now I was confused. If everything was up to me, what was I paying the most famous psychoanalyst in New Mouse City to do? "Will this treatment be expensive?" I asked.

"HOW SERIOUS IS IT?"

The doctor stood up. "Vell, it could be expensive," he said. "Or it could not be. Zis is up to you!"

This rodent was beginning to sound like a broken record. Just then, he put his paw on my shoulder. "Remember, zis is all up to you!" he repeated. "You must **FACE YOUR FEARS**. Otherwise you vill never get vell. I vill see you next Vednesday. For now, it vill be vone hundred dollars. Thank you."

I left Dr. Shrinkfur's office feeling much lighter. That's because my wallet was completely empty!

I left Dr. Shrinkfur's office feeling much lighter.

Well, if the most famous **PSYCHOANALYST** in **NEW MOUSE CITY** said it was up to me to get well, then I guess it was!

WHAT'S UP, GERONIMO?

For the next few days, I couldn't leave the house. What if it rained? What if a giant cat with two heads attacked me?

Yes, I had to face the fact that I was getting worse. I was **AFRAID** of everything.

Then one morning the phone rang.

"Hello, Stilton speaking, *Geronimo Stilton*," I murmured.

It was my sister, Thea. She is a special correspondent for the newspaper I run, *The Rodent's Gazette.* It is Mouse Island's most popular paper!

"Geronimo!!! *Where have you been?*" squeaked my

sister. "It's been days since you were in the office!" I could tell she was annoyed. "Did you forget about the two television interviews? And what about the conference at the *Press Club*? Have you lost your calendar? Or maybe you're just turning into a cheesebrain!" I could hear her thumping her paw angrily on the desk. Uh-oh. When my sister gets mad, she's like my uncle Cheesebelly when the deli runs out of mozzarella balls. There's no calming her down.

"Um, well, you see," I mumbled, "I wasn't feeling too well. But I'll be there tomorrow. Yes, tomorrow, for sure. . . ."

ALL IN THIRTY SECONDS FLAT!

The next day, I made a decision. It was time to get off my tail. I couldn't stay inside forever. I took a deep breath and forced myself to leave the house.

I took the stairs. No, I wasn't ready for the elevator yet. (I was too **AFRAID** of closed spaces.) Then I opened the front door and stuck my snout outside. It was so noisy! I could barely hear myself think. Car horns blared. Delivery trucks rumbled down the street. Had it always been this loud? Carefully, I set a paw on the pavement. Nothing happened. I was so relieved. **I DID IT! I REALLY DID IT!** Why was I so afraid to go out? It's no big

deal. At last, things were starting to look up.
I walked to the newsstand to buy a paper.

1. I had hardly opened it when . . .

2. A flowerpot fell from a window ledge,
hitting me on the head.

3. Stumbling, I crashed right
into a lamppost.

4. Then I tripped on a mouse
hole cover.

5. I fell and bashed my snout
on the hard pavement.

6. As I was getting up, a taxi ran over my tail.

7. Then a pigeon decided to poop on my nose.

And it all happened in thirty seconds flat! "**Heeeeeeeelp!**" I shrieked in a panic. I immediately scampered back home.

"See, I was right all along!" I squeaked out loud. "Going out is DANGEROUS BUSINESS! From now on, I'm staying put!" I locked the door. It took a little while. I had added five extra dead bolts. You can never be too safe.

No Shots, Please!

Thea called again the next day. She was at the office, even though it was a Sunday. "Geronimo! How are you?" she asked.

"Well, um, I've got a cold," I murmured. I pretended to *SNEEZE*.

There was silence on the other end. Could my sister tell I was faking? "Well, don't worry," she finally squeaked. "We'll just run you right over to Dr. Goodpaws. He'll give you something to get rid of your cold. Maybe a couple of shots will do the trick!"

My eyes nearly popped out of my fur. "*Nooooooooo!*" I shrieked in terror. "No shots, please! I'm already feeling much better. I just need to relax at home for a few more days. You know, unwind."

My sister put me on squeakerphone.

More silence from the other end. Uh-oh. My sister wasn't buying it.

"So I heard you went to see Dr. Shrinkfur," she murmured at last. "Do you have a problem, Geronimo?"

I heard another voice in the background. "Geronimo has a problem? Maybe he should get his snout out of those books. That mouse is too brainy for his own good!"

I groaned. It was my annoying cousin Trap. He runs a thrift store called Cheap Junk for Less. He tells the worst jokes. And he loves to play tricks on me.

Then I heard another, smaller voice. "What's the matter with Uncle Geronimo? Can I say hello to him?" it SQUeaKeD. I smiled. It was my favorite nephew, Benjamin.

The next thing I knew, my sister had put me on squeakerphone. "Go ahead, tell us everything, Geronimo!" she demanded.

I chewed my whiskers. "Well, I went to see Dr. Shrinkfur because I sort of have a little problem . . ." I began.

When I was done talking, Trap was the first to pipe up.

"So what did Dr. Shrinky Dink tell you to do?" he asked.

I told him about the doctor's advice. If I wanted to get rid of my fears, I had to face them . . . only, I was too afraid to start!

If I wanted to get rid of my fears, I had to face them.

A PACKAGE FOR MR. STILTON!

Half an hour later, the doorbell rang.

Ring! Ring! Ring! Ring!

I decided not to answer it.
But the doorbell kept ringing.

It was ten times worse than the ding of the toaster oven, which I was now afraid of. I wanted to stick my head UNDERWATER to drown out the horrible noise.

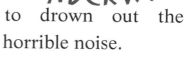

Finally, I went to the door.

"A package for Mr. Stilton!" a small voice squeaked.

I didn't move.

Then I heard a loud sniff. "Hmm . . . this smells like a box of Cheesy Chews to me," the voice continued. "What a lucky mouse!"

Instantly, my mouth began to water.

I scratched my head. I couldn't just leave A BOX of Cheesy Chews on my front step. They would melt for sure. All of that delicious chocolate and cheese gone to waste. It was unthinkable. It was unimaginable. It was unmousy.

I waited for a couple of minutes. Then I carefully unlocked the door.

I stuck my snout outside. . . .

CHEESY CHEWS

Before I could even squeak, six paws grabbed me. They lifted me up and threw me into a car.

"Heeelp!" I shrieked. "I'm being mousenapped!"

Someone started the car. We shot off with **A SQUEAL OF TIRES**. I felt like I was

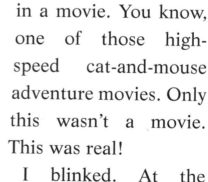

in a movie. You know, one of those high-speed cat-and-mouse adventure movies. Only this wasn't a movie. This was real!

I blinked. At the wheel sat my sister, Thea, with my cousin

Trap at her side. My young nephew Benjamin kept me company in the back.

"BUT I'M AFRAID TO GO OUT!" I shrieked in terror.

Trap squeaked, "OH, DON'T BE SUCH A BABY!" He shoved a Cheesy Chew into my mouth. I wanted to tell him I wasn't a baby. I just had a problem with leaving my house. And with driving in fast cars. And with putting my paws under those paw dryers in public bathrooms. They can be so hot. A mouse could burn his or her fur right off.

But I couldn't say a word. My mouth was full.

Oh, how I love my Cheesy Chews!

Trap was happily squeaking away. "Tell me, Cousinkins," he babbled. "Do you like the dark chocolates with the blue-cheese filling best?

Or the cheddar-and-caramel creams?"

Without waiting for a reply, he shoved another Cheesy Chew into my mouth.

It was so good! My mood was beginning to lift!

Benjamin sat next to me, happily nibbling away. "Look, Uncle Geronimo!" he squeaked. "Here's a CARAMEL SWISS DIP. My favorite!"

He offered a mozzarella-and-marshmallow roll to Thea.

"Try this one, Auntie," he said. "It's yummy!"

I must say, the Cheesy Chews were delicious. We polished them off in a jiffy.

I was so busy munching chocolates

that I lost track of time. Suddenly, the car stopped.

We were at the airport.

MAKE WAY!
MAKE WAAAAAY!

I got out. That's when it hit me. We were at the airport. I hate airports. And not just because I hate to fly. Airports are so crowded and busy. All of those rodents rushing around. It's enough to give me a mouse-sized headache!

"Why have you brought me here?" I asked in a panic.

My cousin Trap winked at me and laughed. "Oh, we're just getting started, Gerrykins," he said mysteriously.

"What do you mean?" I asked. I was beginning to get **WORRIED**. WORRIED WORRIED WORRIED WORRIED WORRIED WORRIED WORRIED

But before I could say another word, Trap shoved me onto a luggage cart. WORRIED

"LET THE FUN AND GAMES BEGIIIIIN!"

he squeaked.

Then he pushed me at breakneck speed through the airport.

"Make way! Make waaaaay!" he screamed with glee. "Don't you just love speeding?"

"Nooooooo!" I wailed in horror. But my cousin was on a roll. And I'm not talking about the rolling luggage cart. Trap was running so fast his paws barely touched the ground. Suddenly, he stopped in front of the **VIR** (VERY IMPORTANT RODENT) waiting lounge.

I HATE GOING FAST!

A pretty female mouse with blonde fur was just coming out. She was wearing a very **TRENDY SAFARI OUTFIT** with a *synthetic cat-fur vest* and a pair of laced-up **LEATHER BOOTS**. A NECKLACE MADE OF SHARK'S TEETH completed the look.

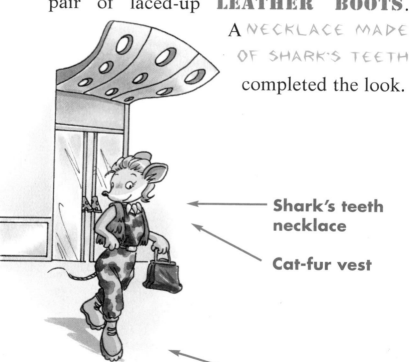

Shark's teeth necklace

Cat-fur vest

Leather boots

SHARK'S TEETH

Trap stopped in front of the stranger.

I smoothed my fur. The pretty mouse seemed to be staring right at me. "Oh, my!" she exclaimed. "Aren't you *Geronimo Stilton*, the famous writer?"

I blushed to the end of my whiskers.

The mouse twirled her shark's teeth necklace. Then she leaned toward me. "Could I have your autograph?" she asked. "I've read all of your books. They're so exciting! I think my favorite one is *The Curse of the Cheese Pyramid*. It made me want to travel to Egypt. I also enjoyed *Cat and Mouse in a Haunted House*. It was gripping! Only a very special mouse could write so well!"

I was flattered. It was so nice to meet a fan. Especially such a pretty one.

I was about to say something clever when Trap took off again. We barreled toward the elevator with a squeal of tires.

WE BARRELED TOWARD THE ELEVATOR WITH A SQUEAL OF TIRES

I'm Afraid
of Elevators!

Minutes later, my cousin dumped me off the luggage cart. I landed in a heap on the floor.

Oops!

"Oops-a-daisy!" Trap chuckled.

I picked myself up. Then I straightened my glasses. My cousin hit a button on the wall next to us. That's when I realized we had made it to the elevator. "No!" I shrieked at the top of my lungs. "I CAN'T GET ON THAT! I'M AFRAID OF ELEVATORS!"

But Trap just twirled his tail. "Don't worry, Gerrykins," he cried. "There's nothing to it. Just don't think about it!"

The elevator doors opened. I tried to run away, but Trap stuck out his paw. I tripped. Before I could stop myself, I had rolled right into the elevator!

Trap hopped in behind me. "See, nothing to it!" he said.

The doors slid shut. I gulped, then closed my eyes. I would never make it!

I was already having problems breathing. My tail was trembling. My whiskers were dripping with sweat.

It doesn't get any worse than this, I thought. But then it did.

Trap stamped on my paw. I shrieked. The pain was horrible.

At last, the doors opened. "No need to thank me," squeaked my cousin happily. "I told you, just don't think about it!"

Trap stamped on my paw.

I'M AFRAID
OF FLYING!

By now, I'd had **ENOUGH**. "Take me back home!" I insisted. "I got on that elevator, but I am not getting on a plane! **I'M AFRAID OF FLYING!**"

As usual, my cousin seemed to ignore me. Instead, he raised his eyebrows. "Look over there!" he whispered in my ear.

It was the pretty mouse we had met earlier. She was standing at the check-in desk. I couldn't help smiling. She really was attractive. And she was a fan of my books. What a great combination! I should have found out her name. Maybe we could be pen pals. Maybe we could share a grilled cheese sandwich at the Squeak & Chew sometime.

I stared dreamily into space. I didn't notice my cousin scamper over to the **MOUSAIR** check-in counter. He returned, waving three tickets in the air.

"Here we are!" he squeaked, waking me out of my daydream. "Thea, Benjamin, and I have seats at the back of the plane. Geronimo, you are in seat 11B."

I shook my head. "B-b-but I can't sit alone," I stammered. "I just told you, I'm afraid of flying!"

Then i heard a soft voice behind me. It was the pretty stranger. "Did you say you are sitting in 11B?" she murmured.

I nodded. "How exciting!" she exclaimed. "I am in 11A. That means we'll sit together!"

I grinned. What a sweet mouse. It would be nice to spend more time with a fan. Maybe I could get on the plane after all.

Beside me, Trap **winked**. For some reason, he looked very pleased with himself.

Pssst!

What was this all about? But there was no time to think. We were about to board.

"By the way, where are we going?" I whispered to Trap as we stood in line.

"Um, yes, well, it's a beautiful place," he mumbled. "Lots of fresh air and sunshine. You're going to love it."

For the first time since I'd been mousenapped, I began to relax. Maybe a little vacation would do me some good. I could sleep until noon. Take a dip in the pool. Watch the sun set over the ocean.

"That's right," Trap continued. "We're headed for **RATTYTRAP JUNGLE** on the RIO MOSQUITO."

My eyes popped open. Rattytrap Jungle? Rio Mosquito? What an odd place for a resort. Oh, well, I sighed. Maybe the mosquitoes were friendlier in the tropics.

YOU'RE A REAL GENIUS!

A few minutes later, we boarded the plane.

I quickly found my seat next to the pretty stranger. "I'm so honored to be sitting next to you," gushed my fan. "YOU ARE A REAL GENIUS. Your books have changed my life!"

I was so flattered I didn't even realize we had taken off.

For the next few hours, I chatted with my new friend. I was having so much fun I forgot all about my fear of flying!

Unfortunately, my obnoxious cousin Trap took that moment to remind me. He began shouting at me through a megaphone.

"Just don't think about it!"

he squeaked at the top of his lungs. The other passengers nearly jumped out of their seats. They shot him murderous looks. But Trap didn't care. He was having too much fun. "Just don't think about it!" he repeated over and over.

For once, I decided to take my cousin's advice. I stopped thinking about flying. Instead, I thought about wringing his neck!

JUST SIGN HERE!

Soon we were landing. My pretty new friend was still chattering away. "Oh, silly me," she laughed. "I almost forgot to introduce myself. My name is **PENELOPE POISONFUR**. But you can call me P.P. for short." She winked.

I grinned. Maybe this would be a good time to mention my pen pal idea. After all, I didn't want to lose touch with P.P. She was one special mouse. But before I had a chance to ask, P.P. began whispering in my ear. "Do you know why I'm going to the Rio Mosquito?" she asked. Then she told me. It seemed Penelope had signed up to take some kind of special

RIO MOSQUITO

course. The course was only open to a few **CHOICE RODENTS**. Suddenly, she grabbed both of my paws. "I just had the greatest idea!" she squeaked. "Why don't you come with me?" She pulled out a piece of paper from her bag. "All you have to do is sign this form!" she added.

I didn't know what to say. I had never met such a bold mouse before. Bold . . . and charming.

"Well, I'm sort of traveling with my family," I began. I glanced at the back of the plane. My cousin was busy launching spitballs into the air. I pictured the vacation. Trap would probably be playing pranks on me the whole time. I'd end up with a knot in my tail and itching powder in my bed. I turned back to my new friend. "What kind of course is it?" I asked.

...OOHHMMM...

P.P. threw her paw around my shoulder. "TRUST ME," she murmured. "IT'S JUST WHAT YOU NEED. YOU'LL FEEL LIKE A NEW MOUSE!"

Now I pictured myself in a lush green tropical paradise. Maybe we would do yoga by the pool. Or some deep-breathing exercises by the soothing ocean.

"Are you sure it's going to be relaxing?" I asked.

"I guarantee it's going to be the best thing for you," P.P. insisted. She smiled flirtatiously.

I was completely charmed.

So I signed.

In a flash, she snatched up the form. For some reason, she had the strangest look on her face. No, it wasn't a smile this time. It was more like a sneer.

"LET THE FUN AND GAMES BEGIN!"

she squeaked.

How very strange, I thought. Where had I heard those same words before?

How very strange!

It's Signed and Sealed, Stilton!

I left the plane. I had to find Thea. I wanted to introduce her to my new friend. I knew she would be thrilled to meet one of my fans. My sister calls me a bookworm, but I know she is proud of my success.

"Thea!" I squeaked happily when I found her. "This is **PENELOPE POISONFUR**. She is a fan who has read all of my books!"

My sister ignored me and turned to Penelope. "Well, *did he sign?*" she asked.

P.P. still had that same strange sneer on her face. *"He signed it, all right!"* she laughed. "It was as easy as taking cheese niblets from a baby!"

My mouth dropped open. What was she

talking about? And why did she sound so mean?

Trap, Thea, and Benjamin were nodding their heads. "*He signed it*," they whispered to one another.

Uh-oh. Something very odd was going on. What were they talking about? And why were they all staring at me? I didn't like it one bit.

"Who is *he*?" I asked, worried. "What did he sign?"

Instead of answering, Thea, Trap, and Benjamin turned toward Penelope. She pointed her paw at me.

"YOU have signed it, Stilton!" she shouted at the top of her lungs.

IT'S TOO LATE, STILTON!

I gulped. What was going on? "But, P.P.," I protested. "I don't understand. What did I sign?"

Penelope held up her paw in front of my face. "First of all," she yelled, "forget the P.P. From now on, I'm Ms. Poisonfur to you!"

My mouth dropped open in shock. She'd seemed like such a sweet mouse on the plane.

"Don't look so surprised, Stilton!" Ms. Poisonfur **barked**. "Just do as you're told and don't make a squeak. Now get on that jeep!" She pointed to a YELLOW TRUCK parked by the plane.

I blinked. This was getting ridiculous. Who was this mouse? And why was she

screaming at me? Before I could ask, she shoved a piece of paper in my face. It was the form that I had signed on the plane.

"It's too late, Stilton, you've already signed!" Penelope squeaked.

I was beginning to get a terrible feeling in my stomach. I glanced at the form. It read:

TO THE LAST WHISKER SURVIVAL SCHOOL

"I've signed up for some kind of boot camp!" I screeched. "But I'm not the boot-camp type. I'm afraid of bugs and dirt and things that go squeak in the night. Plus, I look awful in khaki. It's just not my color!"

Oh, what had I gotten myself into this time? I decided I had only one

43

TO THE LAST WHISKER
SURVIVAL SCHOOL

Tarantula Trail 115
Rattytrap Jungle — Rio Mosquito

I, the undersigned, agree to take part in the survival course offered by To the Last Whisker. The course will last for seven days. It will take place in Rattytrap Jungle on the Rio Mosquito.

By signing this form, I agree to obey **without question** all of Ms. Penelope Poisonfur's orders.

Should I refuse to take part in the course or to obey Ms. Poisonfur, I promise to pay a fine of one million dollars.

Signed:

Geronimo Stilton

choice. I'd have to make a run for it. But just as I turned to leave, Penelope grabbed me by the tail.

"Get in the jeep, Stilton!" she ordered. Then she handed me a magnifying glass.

"You haven't read the small print," she smirked.

I read the last line on the form out loud. "Should I refuse to take part in the course or to obey Ms. Poisonfur, I promise to pay a fine of ONE M-M-M-M-MILLION dollars," I stammered. This was outrageous! "But I don't have one million dollars!" I cried. My paws were shaking.

Penelope shot me an evil look. "Exactly!" she sneered. "NOW GET IN THAT JEEP!"

Hhmmm...

"I'LL FIX YOU ALL RIGHT, STILTON!"

I stumbled forward. *I must be having a bad dream,* I thought. I closed my eyes. But when I opened them, Ms. Poisonfur was glaring at me.

My family watched as I climbed into the jeep. "Benjamin," I squeaked. "How could you trick me like this?"

My favorite nephew had tears in his eyes. "Uncle, it's for your own good! I promise!"

Thea nodded her head. "That's right," she chimed in. "You'll thank us."

Trap winked at me. "The week will just fly by, you'll see!" he added.

"Don't worry!" Ms. Poisonfur squeaked. Then she punched me hard in the shoulder. I winced. This was one tough mouse. "I'll fix you!" she sneered.

"I'LL FIX YOU ALL RIGHT, STILTON!"

I'm Afraid of Bugs!

The jeep made its way along a paved road. Soon the road turned into a beaten track. Then it became a **MUDDY** path.

It was so hot I felt like a walking sprinkler. I was dripping sweat! Clouds of mosquitoes swarmed around me. They were having a party in my fur. I figured my tail was their dinner. They were making a meal out of it. What if they gave me some rare disease?

I'M AFRAID OF DISEASES!

We reached the camp in the middle of the night. It looked like an army barracks. It stood in the middle of a clearing surrounded by very tall trees.

I was so tired. I fell onto a smelly bunk bed. I tried not to think about the fleas that were probably crawling in it. Ugh!

I'M AFRAID OF BUGS!

Exhausted, I fell asleep fully dressed. That night, I kept hearing Trap's voice in my dreams. "Just don't think about it!" he chanted over and over.

DAY 1: MONDAY

At dawn, Penelope gave me a wake-up call. She poured a bucketful of icy water on my head! "**LINE UP!**" she shrieked.

I looked outside. That's when I discovered there were four other mice taking this crazy jungle course.

I was about to slip into the green jumpsuit I'd found in my closet. But, even though I was in the hot jungle, I'd put on a clean undershirt first. I love my undershirts. I wear one all the time, even in the summer. That's because I'M AFRAID OF DRAFTS.

Unfortunately, Penelope was watching me. Before I could put one paw through my undershirt, she snatched it away and squeaked at the top of her lungs,

A GAME FOR REAL MICE

FIND THE ARTICLE OF CLOTHING A REAL MOUSE WOULD NOT WEAR.

① ② ③ ④ ⑤ ⑥

ANSWER:

THE ARTICLE OF CLOTHING A REAL MOUSE WOULD NOT WEAR IS THE UNDERSHIRT (2).

"REAL MICE DON'T WEAR UNDERSHIRTS, STILTON!"

I cringed, then put on the jumpsuit. Penelope threw an enormous backpack at me. It weighed a ton. I'd be lucky if I could take one pawstep.

Meanwhile, Penelope lifted her own backpack without batting an eyelash. Then I followed her outside.

"FORWARD MARCH!" she yelled.

We left **camp** and began our long trek.

I introduced myself to the other mice.

Geronimo Stilton

"Good morning, everyone," I said. "My name is Stilton, *Geronimo Stilton*."

A big, tough, muscled mouse nodded at me. He wore his fur in a crew cut. "I'm Burt Burlyrat. But you can call me B.B.," he announced. "I'm a forest ranger."

Next to B.B. stood a short, round rodent. He clasped my paw. "How do you do, my name is Tubby Tumblemouse," he said. Then he whispered, "My friends call me Furball." I smiled. Tubby seemed like a nice mouse. I wondered why he had signed up for this course.

BURT BURLYRAT, AKA B.B.

Tubby told me he was a **cheese salesmouse**. He had put on a few extra pounds eating too many samples. "I thought this was an easy weight-loss course. Ms. Poisonfur told me it would be like a mini vacation," he explained. Sweat dripped down his fur. "She didn't tell me we'd be forced to run twenty miles a day!"

"W-w-what?" I stammered, sinking under the heavy backpack. "Twenty miles a day? I'm **never** going to make it! I've got low blood pressure! I've got low iron! I've got low self-esteem!" This was going to be worse than I'd thought. "Oh, how did I get myself into this mess?!"

TUBBY TUMBLEMOUSE, AKA FURBALL

I sobbed, burying my snout in my paws.

Tubby put his paw around my shoulder. "Don't panic, Geronimo," he whispered. "I've brought an emergency supply of **cheese sandwiches**. They're hidden in my backpack."

Just then, a teenaged mouse with pigtails scampered over. "Hi, there!" she chirped. "I'm Suzie Squeakers."

Suzie Squeakers

Next came an elderly female rodent. She was small and skinny, with wiry fur. She wore a pair of thick glasses and a *purple baseball cap*. She introduced herself as Sandy Silverfur. Sandy was old, but you wouldn't find her in any old mouse home. Not yet, anyway. Sandy LOVED TO

Sandy Silverfur

LIVE DANGEROUSLY. In fact, you could say she was a bit of a daredevil. She once went scuba diving off the shores of Tomcat Island!

Unlike Sandy and B.B., hiking through the jungle was not my idea of a good time. Within minutes, my paws were covered with blisters.

Suddenly, a **terrible screeching** filled the air. It was Penelope, singing.

"I AM A WILD RODENT,
I HAVE A WILD HEART!
NOTHING EVER SCARES ME,
BECAUSE I'M TOUGH AND SMART!
THIS COURSE IS REALLY SUPER,
YOU LEARN TO BE A TROUPER!
YOU LEARN TO MARCH AND SWEAT AND SING
YOU LEARN TO DO MOST ANYTHING!"

I grumbled. That was the most ridiculous song I had ever heard.

Who likes to march?

But soon the rest of the group was singing along.

Well, you wouldn't catch me joining in. I wasn't into singing. I was having enough trouble just breathing!

Then, someone waved the contract under my snout. It was Penelope.

"You signed it, Stilton. Now sing!" she demanded. "Sing or you'll be sorry!" Her beady little eyes drilled right through me. I shivered. Then I sang at the top of my lungs.

I was so busy singing I hardly noticed we had entered the forest. Trees as tall as

Snap snap snap!

skyscrapers surrounded us. The foliage was **so thick** we couldn't see any sunlight. The trees were home to all kinds of animals. They called to one another as we

passed by. Monkeys, parrots, cheetahs, and snakes watched our every move. We were like rodent celebrities at an awards show. Only no one was snapping our picture.

Instead, they were snapping their teeth! This tropical jungle was a very scary place. One wrong pawstep and we'd all be history!

WE MARCHED AND MARCHED AND MARCHED AND MARCHED.

And then? WE MARCHED some more.

We didn't even stop for a meal. Instead, Penelope handed out sandwiches as we hiked. Unfortunately, they were not cheese sandwiches. They were made of mashed fleas. I had never seen anything so gross in my life. Some of the fleas were still kicking their tiny legs. I was so disgusted. But I was so hungry. I ate every bite.

We were allowed to stop only to go to the bathroom. Penelope timed us. Fifteen seconds for each mouse. For any other emergency, we had to hand in a written request.

I quickly jotted down a note. "Dear Ms.

All kinds of animals...

Snap!

...watched our every move.

Snap!

Snap!

nap!

Snap!

ap!

Snap!

nap!

Snap!

nap!

Snap!

nap!

Snap!

nap!

Snap!

A very scary place...   ...we'd all be history!   Snap!

Snap!   Snap!

Poisonfur," it read. "Would it be possible to take a short break?"

Penelope read the note out loud, then laughed. "You city rodents are spineless," she smirked. "You're as soft as a bowl of cheese with extra cream, Stilton!" She twirled her tail, deep in thought. "This may be harder than I thought," she murmured. "But don't worry. I'll fix you. When you're done with this course, you'll be stronger than a maximum-strength glue trap. And best of all, you'll be smarter than the sharpest street mouse in all of New Mouse City!"

We marched for the rest of the day. When it turned dark, the jungle became even more **TERRIFYING**. Spooky shadows were everywhere. Strange eyes glowed in the

eyes glowed in the trees.

trees. Night birds sang to one another. And I'm not talking happy jingles. These songs sounded more like creepy Halloween music. Worst of all, it was dark. Very dark.

Did I mention . . .

I'M AFRAID OF THE DARK?

But I was forced to forget about it. I had to put one paw in front of the other. I had no choice. Finally, at midnight, we stopped. We were so tired.

We sat down *AROUND A FIRE*.

"Come and get it!" shouted Penelope, banging on a pot with a spoon.

I was starving. I grabbed my bowl and began to slurp up the reddish liquid. Seconds later, I started to gag. "Bleah!!!! What's this?" I cried.

Penelope sneered. "That's red-ant soup, Stilton!" she squeaked.

"EAT IT OR YOU'LL BE SORRY!"

The rest of us looked at one another. We looked at the soup. Then we looked at Penelope. She glared at us, her paws planted firmly on her hips. The soup looked scary. But Penelope looked like a rabid cat about to go on a hunting spree.

Like robots, we picked up our spoons and ate. I was so tired I could hardly chew.

Later, I **FELL ASLEEP** with my snout in my bowl. Oh, well. At least no one was bothered by my snoring.

I fell asleep with my snout in my bowl.

Day 2: Tuesday

The next morning, Penelope woke me up with another bucketful of icy water. "**LINE UP!**" she yelled. Hadn't she ever heard of an alarm clock?

After a breakfast of grilled beetles, we continued our marching. We marched nonstop until noon. I was hoping Penelope had decided to give us a break. But instead,

Splash!

she gave us a crash course in first aid. I must admit, she taught us some pretty neat things. We even learned mouse-to-mouse resuscitation.

I guess we were all doing okay until lunch. That's when Tubby lost it. After eating his snailburger, he decided TO DIG INTO his secret supply of cheese sandwiches. But before he could take a single bite, Penelope caught him. She threw all of the sandwiches into the river.

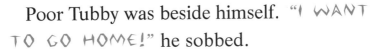

Poor Tubby was beside himself. "I WANT TO GO HOME!" he sobbed.

But Penelope just waved the contract under his snout. "Too late, Tubster!" she shrieked. "You signed it!"

In a sudden fit, Tubby snatched the paper from her paw. Then he shoved it in his mouth and chewed it up. He looked so pleased with himself.

But Tubby's excitement didn't last long. In a flash, Penelope had pulled out another

Crunch crunch crunch!

Ha-ha-haaa!

contract from her backpack. "That was just a copy, Tubby Tails," she chuckled. "I have the original in my office!"

Tubby's whiskers drooped. He hung his head. His tail dragged on the ground. I had never seen a mouse look so beaten. "Here, have my snailburger!" I insisted. "I'll skip lunch."

Tubby thanked me with tears in his eyes. "Geronimo, you are a true friend. I will never forget you," he cried.

After lunch, it was back to marching. At last, we reached the Rio Mosquito.

A rope hung over the water, stretched between two trees. The river roared downstream, picking up anything in its path. I saw twigs. I saw tree trunks. I saw a houseboat filled with monkeys. Everything was swept away in the raging current.

"I'm scared!" I squeaked. *"I'M AFRAID OF DROWNING!"*

Penelope rolled her eyes. "Get moving or you'll be sorry!" she demanded.

We did as we were told. What choice did we have? I grabbed the rope and began to cross the river. *One paw at a time*, I told myself. Slowly we made our way to the other side. I was doing it!

But suddenly, disaster struck. Someone was crying. "I'm so hungry! I'm going to faint!" Tubby wailed. Seconds later, the rope slipped from his paws. He hit the water with a loud splash. What could I do? I dove in after him.

Tubby's snout was already underwater. I quickly grabbed hold of his tail. Groaning, I dragged him onto the bank. Then I gave him mouse-to-mouse resuscitation. It worked!

"Thank you! You saved my life!" squeaked a grateful Tubby.

I grinned. I felt like Supermouse when he does a good deed. Too bad I wasn't really Supermouse. If I were, I could have flown right home! Still, I was proud of myself for facing another fear.

I guess Penelope was proud of me, too. "You're learning, Stilton!" she sniggered. "You're learning!"

DAY 3: WEDNESDAY

"Today is a day of rest!" shouted Penelope the next morning. As usual, she had woken us up with a bucketful of icy water.

"Today we will build a tree house," Penelope continued. "Stilton, you'll be the first one to climb that tree over there!"

She pointed to a tree. It wasn't just any old tree. It was the tallest tree I had ever seen in my life! Up, up, up it went. I got dizzy just looking at it.

"I c-can't climb that t-t-tree!" I stammered. "I'M AFRAID OF HEIGHTS!"

Just then, a small paw tapped my shoulder. It was Suzie Squeakers.

"Don't worry," she whispered. "I'm a friend of **Pinky Pick**. She sent me along to help you." Suzie handed me a pink envelope. It was a letter from Pinky.

Have I told you about Pinky Pick? She's a young assistant at my office. I'm sure you can guess Pinky's favorite color. It's pink, of course! Pinky has pink sneakers and rides a pink bicycle to work. She will only write on pink paper and loves squeaking on her pink cell phone. I guess

Pinky Pick

Assistant to the Boss

DEAR BOSS,

You can trust Suzie Squeakers. She's my best friend.

Suzie is a Gerbil Scout. She got her wilderness badge last year.

She spent one whole night in the woods outside her mouse hole!

Good luck!

Pinky Pick

P.S. If you make it back alive, can I have a pink computer?

**The Rodent's Gazette
17 Swiss Cheese Center
New Mouse City, Mouse Island 13131**

www.geronimostilton.com

Pinky Pick

you could say Pinky is sort of hung up on the color pink. One winter, she lost her favorite pink mittens. She had to wear blue ones instead. Poor Pinky cried for weeks!

Now I bent over Pinky's letter.

Suzie winked at me. When Penelope wasn't looking, she began to follow me up the tree. Immediately, I felt faint. "Don't look down!" Suzie advised. It was good advice. If I didn't look down, I couldn't tell how high up we had climbed.

I breathed a sigh of relief. This was no big deal. We were only a few feet off the ground. I probably could have jumped down if I'd

wanted to. I pretended I was climbing up the steps to my mouse hole. Oh, it would be so nice to be home! Home with my cheese-filled fridge. Home with my treasured books.

I glanced down at my paws. Big mistake. No, I wasn't at home. Far from it. I was up so high even Penelope Poisonfur looked harmless. My head began to spinnnnnn. I was going to fall! Newspaper headlines flashed before my eyes. **Geronimo Stilton Killed in a Terrible Fall! Jungle Terrorizes Publisher! Stilton's Last Squeak!**

Just then, someone grabbed my tail. It was Suzie. "It's okay!" she shrieked. "I got you!"

I was so happy I could have jumped for

joy. Luckily, I remembered where I was just in time. I was happy, but I wasn't a cheesehead. I wasn't about to let go of that tree!

At last, we came to a very long branch with thick leaves. "This is the perfect spot to build our shelter," announced Suzie. Together we built a ladder out of some tree limbs. Before long, our tree house was looking great. *I was so proud of myself and my new friends.* And best of all, I realized being up so high wasn't that scary after all.

"Not bad for a bunch of city mice," Penelope admitted when we were finished. "Not bad at all . . . "

That night I dreamed that Pinky Pick was winking at me. "What do you say, BOSS?" she squeaked. "Can I have that pink computer now? Can I, Boss?"

DAY 4: THURSDAY

The next morning, I woke up to a pair of singing birds. The sun warmed my fur. I stretched. For the first time since I'd arrived in the jungle, I felt great. But what was different about today? I just couldn't put my paw on it. Then it hit me—**a bucketful of icy water** right in my snout!

Penelope Poisonfur snickered, then she barked out orders. "LINE UP! she squeaked. "Today you will learn to use a compass. Each of you must find your way to our next **CAMPSITE** before nightfall. And you must do it on your own!"

I shuddered.

"BUT I'M AFRAID TO BE LEFT ON MY OWN IN THE FOREST

I cried. Too late. Everyone had already left.

I was alone in the forest. This was worse than the time I got separated from my uncle Nibbles at the Marvelous Mouse Tail Circus. At least that time, the rat clowns kept me laughing. Now there wasn't a rodent in sight. Monkeys **SHRIEKED** at me from the trees. Snakes **HISSED** from behind rocks. Even the singing birds sounded **SCARY**. I jumped at every noise. I was like a furry rubber band ready to snap.

I decided I'd better study the map. *This will be as easy as cheesepie,* I told myself. All I had to do was figure out how to get to the camp. "Um, let's see," I mumbled. "I am here, or maybe I'm here. And then I'm headed there — or maybe there?" I checked the compass. North, South, East, West. It wasn't as easy as I'd thought. I tried giving myself a pep talk. "You can figure it out, Stilton," I insisted. "Just use your brain!" But my brain must have been taking a cheese break. Half an hour later, I burst into tears. "Rotten rat's teeth!" I squeaked. "I'm lost!"

I roamed the jungle for hours. Every now and then, I would stop to have a good cry. Oh, how could my family do this to me? They said they wanted to help me, but maybe they just wanted to get rid of me! Yes, that had to be it! If I were gone, my sister would probably sell *The Rodent's Gazette*. She'd buy a beauty salon and get her fur done every day for free. My cousin would move into my large, comfy mouse hole. He was such a slob. He'd make a mess of my

SUDDENLY, I HEARD A RUSTLING SOUND IN THE LEAVES.

pretty cat-fur rug. Just thinking about it made me angry. "I'm going to make it back if it kills me!" I cried, stamping my paw.

Suddenly, I heard a rustling sound in the leaves. I gulped. Maybe I shouldn't have used the word *kill*. I didn't want to give some wild animal any ideas!

Grabbing a big stick for protection, I hid behind a tree.

Just then, I saw a bush move.

"Take that, you wild animal!" I shrieked, striking with all my might.

"**Oooouch!**" a voice cried out.

Bang!

Geronimo Stilton

"Oooouch!"

Burt Burlyrat

A rodent crawled out from behind the bush.
No, it wasn't a wild animal at all. It was
Burt Burlyrat.

"Oh, I'm so sorry, B.B.!" I apologized. "I
thought you were about to attack me!"

Burt rubbed his head. He looked annoyed.

By now, he had sprouted a huge bump on his forehead. I felt bad about the bump. But I didn't feel bad about running into B.B. With his help, I could definitely get to the **NEW CAMP**. After all, B.B. had said he was a forest ranger. A forest ranger should be able

"THE COMPASS IS NEVER WRONG!!!!!"

to read a map and a compass, right?

"*Let's get going!*" he ordered, sounding like an army general. I hopped to my paws. B.B. checked the compass. "This way!" he shouted, storming off. "The compass is never wrong!"

I scurried behind him. B.B. wasn't exactly the friendliest mouse around. I mean, I wouldn't invite him over for one of my aunt Honeywhisker's yummy cheddar casseroles. But I didn't care. I just wanted to get out of this creepy jungle.

After a while, I started to WORRY again. We had been hiking for five hours, but we didn't seem to be getting anywhere. "*Um, B.B., shouldn't we be there by now?*" I asked, wiping sweat from my fur.

He shot me a look. "I told you, Stilton, this is the right direction!" he shrieked.

"The compass is never wrong!"

After **TWO MORE HOURS**, my paws were killing me. B.B. kept insisting we were going the right way, but I had a terrible feeling. Something wasn't right. Finally, the sun began to set. I started to panic. "*Um*, are you sure you know where we're going?" I asked B.B. for the millionth time.

Instead of scowling at me, B.B began to tremble. Then he did the most un-B.B.-like thing. He began to cry! He cried so hard I

thought we would have to swim out of there. "I'm lost!" he choked. "I'm totally and completely lost!"

I tried to cheer him up. "Don't worry," I said. "We are lost together. We'll find our way out of here. I promise."

I stared at the trees surrounding us. All of a sudden, I had an idea. "Let's climb a tree!" I said. "From way up high, we may be able to see our **CAMP!**"

B.B. brightened. Then he turned sad again. "I can't climb a tree," he groaned. "My head is still spinning from the bump. You are the only one who can save us, Geronimo!"

I was worried. But I couldn't let B.B. down. "No problemo," I said, trying to sound brave.

I began to climb. My paws felt like cream

I began to climb.

cheese, but I remembered Suzie Squeaker's advice. I never looked down.

I climbed higher and higher.

After a while, I stopped. I stared out over the treetops.

There! In the dark, I could see the lights from the **CAMP**. I was so happy. I felt like I had just been named author of the year.

"I can see the camp. It's over there!" I called to B.B.

Slowly, I climbed down again. As soon as I reached the ground, B.B. hugged me. It turns out he wasn't a real forest ranger after all. He was just a pretend forest ranger at Mouseyworld, the popular rodents' amusement park. That explained why he couldn't figure out the compass.

Fifteen minutes later, we reached the **CAMP**.

DAY 5: FRIDAY

Penelope **woke us up at dawn** with the usual shower of icy water. I was beginning to wonder where she was getting it. I hadn't had a nice, icy beverage since we left New Mouse City!

After a breakfast of scrambled worms, she gave us a lesson on survival techniques. **"RATTYTRAP JUNGLE IS FULL OF DANGERS!"** she squeaked. "You must be careful where you step, as you are about to see."

She stuck a red flag in the ground. **"SIT HERE, STILTON!"** she ordered.

I was about to sit down when Penelope began to shout, **"DON'T MOVE, STILTON!"** She kicked away a leaf on the ground.

Underneath lay a huge scorpion!

Underneath lay a huge scorpion!

"Be careful where you step," our teacher repeated. "If you had sat down, you'd be **A DEAD MOUSE, STILTON!**"

I shivered. My life flashed before my eyes.

Then, suddenly, someone was poking me. "No time for daydreaming!" Penelope shouted. She pointed to the path ahead. "Danger is everywhere," she said again. "Now walk to the end of the path, Stilton!"

I set out. I had hardly taken more than a couple of steps when I was suddenly lifted into the air! A rope was hidden in the bushes. *It was a trap!*

"Cheese niblets!" I cried. I was dangling upside down!

Our teacher chuckled. "See what I mean, Stilton?" she said, cutting the rope that was holding me up. I fell right on my snout!

"**OW!**" I screamed.

But Penelope wasn't finished with me. "Run toward that tree, Stilton!" she demanded.

I groaned. What would happen to me this time? Would I be blinded by a sharp tree branch? Would I break all of my paws?

I sighed. Then I took off. Seconds later, I fell into a deep, dark hole. "*HELP!*" I shrieked. Our teacher peeped into the hole.

"ARE YOU STILL ALIVE, STILTON?"

she smirked. "Good. Deal with it!" Then she turned to the others. "I hope that you will all remember what has happened to our friend here today!" she squeaked. "Now let's go!"

My mouth dropped open. I began to shake. This was the lowest of the low. How could she leave me alone in this dark, scary place? It was so horrifying. Can you guess why? That's right, I'M AFRAID OF ENCLOSED SPACES!

I waited three hours. Finally, Penelope came back and pulled me out. I was still shaking, but I was proud of myself. I had done it! Yes, I, *Geronimo Stilton*, had faced another fear!

Our teacher peeped into the hole.

Day 6: Saturday

The next morning, I got up extra early. I hid behind my cabin door. I was going to trick our evil teacher at her own game. When she arrived with her bucket of icy water, I stuck out my paw. She tripped. Water flew everywhere. But not a drop landed on me. "*Oops*," I said when Penelope caught me.

She handed me a mop. "**CLEAN UP THIS MESS!**" she ordered, but she was half smiling. "Not bad, Stilton," she admitted. "Not bad for a scaredy mouse."

After a breakfast of fried fleas, we lined up. Penelope said she needed a volunteer. Someone who was afraid of spiders.

I quickly hid behind B.B. I'm sure you

already know why. I AM AFRAID OF SPIDERS!

"I'm going to choose a name," our teacher announced. She stared up at the clouds. She pretended to be deep in thought. But she didn't fool me. I knew what was coming. Seconds later, she cried, "Stilton!"

Oh, *why* did she *always* have to pick on me?! I sighed and came forward.

Penelope picked up a small cage. It was **full of hairy spiders**. Stale Swiss rolls! Just seeing all of those spindly legs gave me **MOUSE BUMPS!**

"Just remember to stay calm," she advised. "Now close your eyes, Stilton!" She placed something on my snout.

"Keep very still, Stilton," our teacher whispered. "And whatever you do, don't open your eyes!"

I tried. But I was curious. I just had to see what was on my snout. Slowly, I peeked open one eye. *AN ENORMOUS HAIRY SPIDER STARED BACK AT ME!*

I was too horrified to squeak.

"Keep still for ten seconds," Penelope ordered. Then she began to count. The rest of the group joined in. "Ten, nine, eight, seven, six, five . . ."

MY WHISKERS TREMBLED WITH FEAR.

"You can do it!" Tubby shouted.

"You're almost there!" B.B. cheered.

"Hurray for Stilton!" everyone shouted when the countdown was over.

I pointed to the spider with a trembling paw. "Take it off, please," I squeaked.

Our teacher sneered. She took the spider and waved it under my nose. How strange. The spider's legs didn't seem to be moving at all. In fact, it looked quite stiff. I peered at it closely.

"It's plastic, Stilton!" Penelope smirked.

I fainted. But moments later, she woke me up with a bucketful of icy water! So

much for starting my day off on the right paw.

Next, Penelope pulled a **huge green snake** from a sack. She twisted it up into a ball like a pro. "I'm going to teach you how to tell the difference between a poisonous snake and one that is harmless," she said. "The one I'm holding now is harmless. Catch it, Silverfur!" she shouted, throwing it to Sandy.

The old mouse went pale, but she still managed to catch that snake in midair.

The reptile twisted itself around her neck. Without batting an eyelash, Sandy shouted, "Yip-peeee!"

Everyone applauded.

Penelope grabbed another snake from the sack. She whirled it in the air. "Always hold a snake by its tail," she explained. "This way it can't bite."

I watched carefully. It looked so easy. Without thinking, I picked up a snake that looked just like the others. I began whirling it over my head.

"Look at me!" I shouted with pride.

For some odd reason, Penelope didn't look happy. Maybe she liked to be the only one showing off. Oh, well, I decided, old Poisonfur would just have to get used to it. The new *Geronimo Stilton* was brave. He was tough. And he wasn't afraid to show it! Then I noticed Penelope had dropped her snake. She waved her paws in the air. What was she doing? Some kind of jungle dance?

"That's the wrong snake, Stilton!"

I began whirling the snake over my head.

Penelope squeaked. "It's poisonous!"

Moldy mozzarella sticks! I was terrified.

"Don't panic, Stilton," our teacher continued. "Just keep whirling it!"

My knees wobbled. My fur stood on end. Still, I managed to keep whirling the snake.

Penelope began playing a tune on her flute.

The snake closed its eyes. Soon it fell asleep.

I wished I was sleeping, too. Old Poisonfur had started yelling at me. Then she picked me up and began whirling *me* over her head!

"NOW YOU'LL LEARN, STILTON!"

Oh, what a day in the jungle!

DAY 7: SUNDAY

Saturday night, we marched nonstop. On Sunday morning, we reached our **FIRST CAMP**. We had only been gone for one week. Still, it felt like a lifetime. **I had learned so much!** Yes, I had to admit, the course in the jungle had changed my life.

After our final bug breakfast, we said our good-byes. *I was sad to see my new friends go.* We had been through so much together.

Tubby hugged me. "Thank you, Geronimo," he said.

"If it weren't for you, I'd be at the bottom of a river!"

Suzie Squeakers winked at me. "It was great to meet you, Boss! Pinky would be proud of you!" she grinned.

Burt Burlyrat crushed my paw in his strong grip. And Sandy Silverfur gave me a photo of me whirling the snake.

"So you won't **forget this course**," she chuckled.

I grinned. I knew I would never forget my adventures in the jungle. Or the friends I had made.

I invited them all to New Mouse City. Finally, it was Penelope's turn. "I've fixed you, haven't I, Stilton?" she smirked.

I shook her paw. I wasn't about to argue. Penelope had cured me. I felt like a new mouse. I wasn't afraid of anything anymore. I could swim in wild rivers. I could climb trees as tall as skyscrapers. I could even eat bug sandwiches. Of course, I didn't have to like them. From now on, I'd be sticking to my favorite kind of sandwiches. The ones with cheese! Like grilled cheese on rye, ham and cheese on a hard roll, and cream cheese and jelly on whole wheat.

I turned around to leave, then shouted,

"THANK YOU, MS. POISONFUR!"

Penelope waved. "You can call me P.P.," she giggled. She really was one special mouse. Maybe someday I could take her out to dinner after all. As long as she didn't order any bugs. Or make me take her mountain climbing course!

Suddenly, I was surrounded by my family. Thea, Trap, and Benjamin were a sight for sore eyes. I hadn't realized how much I had missed them. Yes, I know my sister can be bossy at times. And my cousin loves to play pranks on me. But they're still family.

Just then, my nephew threw his paws around my neck. "Are you still angry with me, Uncle Geronimo?" Benjamin asked.

I stroked his tiny ears and grinned. "Of course not, my little mousey," I sighed. "I love you too much!"

Then I hugged Thea and Trap, too.

"You were right, Stiltons," I said. "This course was the best thing for me. I'm cured!"

The same yellow jeep took us back to the airport from **CAMP**. Then we boarded a plane to New Mouse City. I couldn't wait to get there.

As we were flying home, I thought about everything that had happened to me. I had faced my fears and I had met **four** great new friends. **Five**, if you counted Penelope! Yes, this experience had taught me a lot of things. Like it's much easier to overcome a problem if you tackle it together. And a bucketful of icy water is a terrible way to wake up in the morning!

TELL ME
EFERYTHING, PLEASE!

The next morning, I went to see Dr. Shrinkfur. "Tell me eferything, please!" he insisted.

"You were right, Doctor!" I squeaked. "I went to the Rattytrap Jungle and faced all of my fears. I'm cured!"

He seemed very pleased: "I told you it vas all up to you! Ach, my niece is very clever!" he murmured.

I sat up straight. **"Ms. Poisonfur is your niece?"** I asked.

"Yes, vell, it vas I who gave her name to your relatifes," he confessed. "I vas sure it vould vork. Penelope's style can be a little vacky, but I knew she vas the only vone who could help you."

Fear of the dark!

Snakes!

Heights!

Scorpions!

Spiders!

IT ALL BOILS DOWN TO THIS . . .

So I guess that's the end of my story. It really all boils down to this:

I'm no longer afraid of FLYING!

I'm no longer afraid of the **DARK**!

I'm no longer afraid of **SPIDERS**!

I'm no longer afraid of SNAKES!

As I said, I'm cured!

I'M NOT AFRAID!

I'M NOT AFRAID!

I'M NOT AFRAID!

Oh, well, there is still one thing.

I'm not afraid!

I'm still afraid of **CATS**!

But then again, Dr. Shrinkfur says that's perfectly normal. After all, I am a mouse!

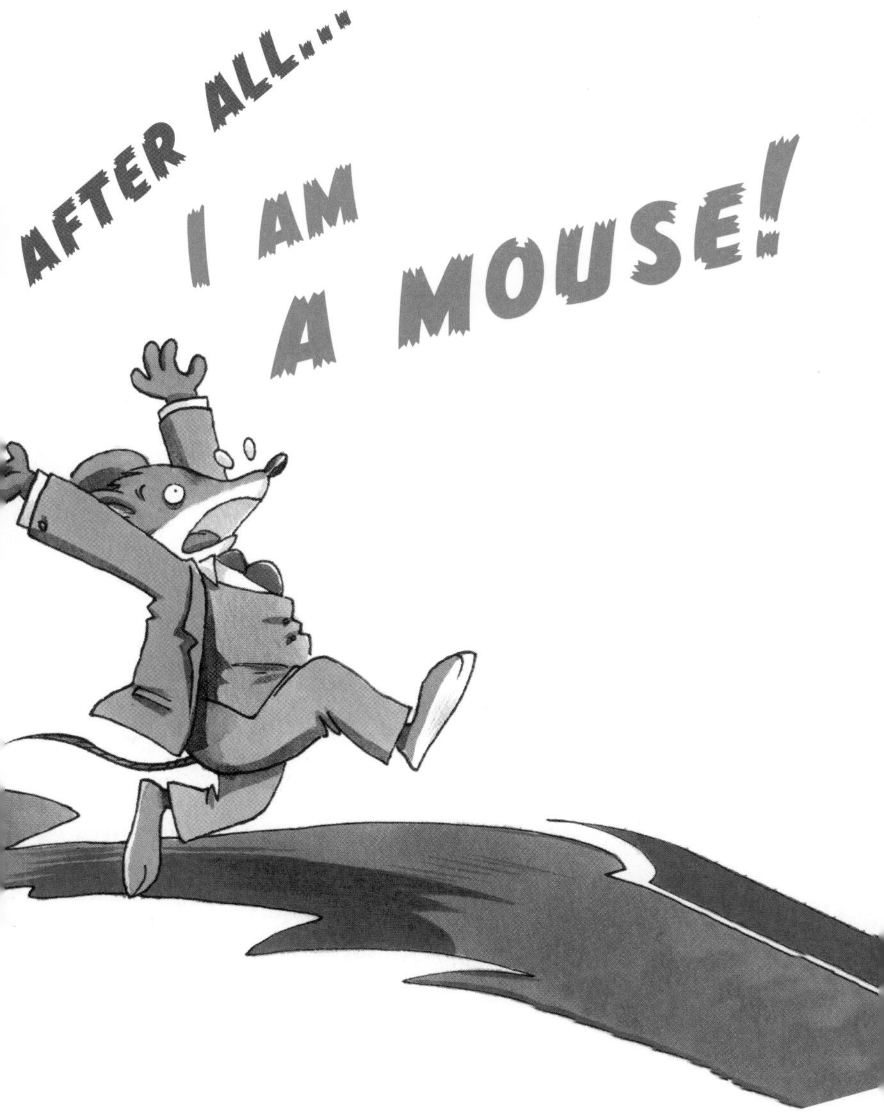
AFTER ALL...
I AM
A MOUSE!

ABOUT THE AUTHOR

Born in New Mouse City, Mouse Island, Geronimo Stilton is Rattus Emeritus of Mousomorphic Literature and of Neo-Ratonic Comparative Philosophy. For the past twenty years, he has been running *The Rodent's Gazette*, New Mouse City's most widely read daily newspaper.

Stilton was awarded the Ratitzer Prize for his scoop on *The Curse of the Cheese Pyramid*. He has also received the Andersen 2000 Prize for Personality of the Year. One of his bestsellers won the 2002 eBook Award for world's best ratlings' electronic book. His works have been published all over the globe.

In his spare time, Mr. Stilton collects antique cheese rinds and plays golf. But what he most enjoys is telling stories to his nephew Benjamin.

Don't miss any of my fabumouse adventures!

Want to read my next adventure?
It's sure to be a fur-raising experience!

PAWS OFF, CHEDDARFACE!

Holey cheese, it was strange! Rodents kept telling me I'd done things I had no memory of. Was I going crazy? Had the cheese finally slipped off my cracker? No, I soon discovered the truth: There was a Geronimo lookalike going around, pretending to be me! Worst of all, he was trying to take over *The Rodent's Gazette*! I had to get that greedy impostor's paws off my newspaper — but how?

THE RODENT'S GAZETTE

1. **Main Entrance**
2. **Printing presses (where the books and newspaper are printed)**
3. **Accounts department**
4. **Editorial room (where the editors, illustrators, and designers work)**
5. **Geronimo Stilton's office**
6. **Storage space for Geronimo's books**

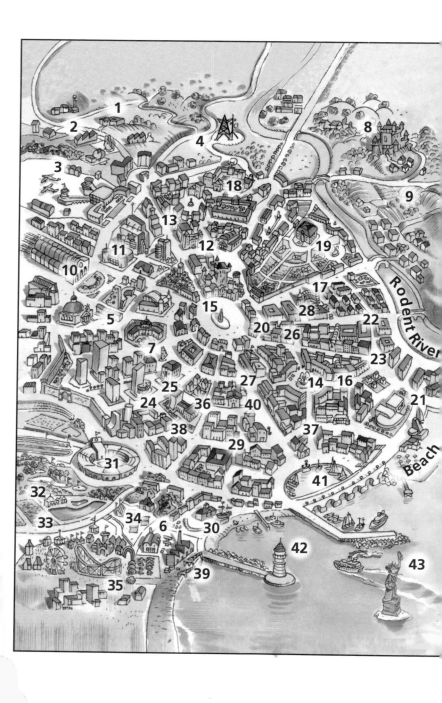

Map of New Mouse City

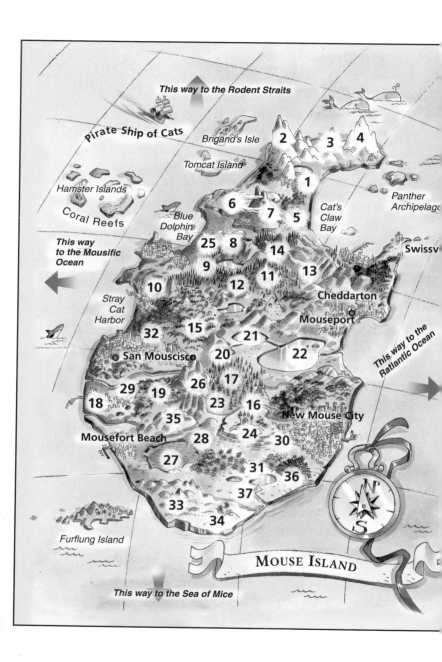

Map of Mouse Island

Dear mouse friends,
thanks for reading, and farewell
till the next book.
It'll be another whisker-licking-good
adventure, and that's a promise!

Geronimo Stilton